Oliver's mum always told him to come straight home after band practice. Dinner was at six o'clock sharp.

As usual, he waited for
the bus with his friends.

But, this evening, something odd happened.

All his friends ran off
before the bus arrived.

"How strange," thought
Oliver James.

And when the bus
did turn up . . .

. . . it didn't stop!

"How will I get home now?" sighed Oliver James.

Eventually, a man came up to the bus stop.
"Excuse me, mister," said Oliver,
"do you know what time
the next bus goes?"

But the man just shouted,
"HELP! A WEREWOLF!"
and ran away.

"A werewolf?"
said Oliver James.
"Where?"

But how had that happened?

It was just so . . .

Suddenly, Oliver James could run

SUPER-FAST.

He could leap **SUPER-HIGH.**

He was

SUPER-STRONG.

But, look! He wouldn't even have to wait that long! There was his friend, Sam, coming round the corner.

"Hey, Sam!" shouted Oliver. "You'll never guess what!"

But Sam just shouted,

"HELP! A WEREWOLF!" and ran away.

"Don't be scared!" cried Oliver. "It's only me!"

PECKNOLD'S

Just then, the clock on
the corner struck six.
Oliver had forgotten
all about the time.

"Oh, no!" he said.
"Dinner's at six o'clock sharp.
I'm going to be late!"

Oliver James raced home at
SUPERNATURAL SPEED.

Seconds later, he skidded to a halt
outside his house. He was home . . .

. . . but could he really go in?
"What if my parents are
frightened of me, too?"

But he was late for dinner,
and his mum would be cross.
So he took a deep breath –

– and went inside.

And what an **AMAZING** surprise!
His mum and dad weren't frightened of
him at all.

"How was band practice?" said Dad.
"Dinner's ready," said Mum.
"You must be hungry."
"I am," said Oliver James.

And he was still **SUPER-HUNGRY** in the morning, too.